M000189550

She Talks to Beethoven

Adrienne Kennedy

A SAMUEL FRENCH ACTING EDITION

SAMUEL FRENCH
FOUNDED 1830

SAMUELFRENCH.COM
SAMUELFRENCH-LONDON.CO.UK

FOR PRODUCTION ENQUIRIES

UNITED STATES AND CANADA
Info@SamuelFrench.com
1-866-598-8449

UNITED KINGDOM AND EUROPE
Plays@SamuelFrench-London.co.uk
020-7255-4302

Each title is subject to availability from Samuel French, depending
upon country of performance. Please be aware that *SHE TALKS TO
BEETHOVEN* may not be licensed by Samuel French in your territory.
Professional and amateur producers should contact the nearest Samuel
French office or licensing partner to verify availability.

MUSIC USE NOTE

Licensees are solely responsible for obtaining formal written permission from copyright owners to use copyrighted music in the performance of this play and are strongly cautioned to do so. If no such permission is obtained by the licensee, then the licensee must use only original music that the licensee owns and controls. Licensees are solely responsible and liable for all music clearances and shall indemnify the copyright owners of the play(s) and their licensing agent, Samuel French, against any costs, expenses, losses and liabilities arising from the use of music by licensees. Please contact the appropriate music licensing authority in your territory for the rights to any incidental music.

IMPORTANT BILLING AND CREDIT REQUIREMENTS

If you have obtained performance rights to this title, please refer to your licensing agreement for important billing and credit requirements.

SHE TALKS TO BEETHOVEN was first produced by JACK in Brooklyn, New York on January 15, 2012. The performance was directed by Charlotte Brathwaite, with sets by Abigail DeVille, costumes by Dede M. Ayite, lighting by Yi Zhao, projections by Hannah Wasileski, sound by Guillerm E. Brown, and dramaturgy by Kate Atwell. The Production Stage Managers were Julie Ann Arbiter and Gabriel DeLeon. The cast was as follows:

SUZANNE	Natalie Paul
BEETHOVEN	Paul-Robert Pryce

CHARACTERS

LUDWIG VAN BEETHOVEN
SUZANNE ALEXANDER – A Writer

AUTHOR'S NOTES

The music in the piece should equal in length the text. Anonymous diary entries are from actual sources.

First produced by River Arts in Woodstock, New York, and directed by Clinton Turner Davis in June 1989.

For my sons, Adam and Joe, without whose encouragement I could not continue to write.

Scene

(Setting: Accra, Ghana, in 1961, soon after independence. It is early evening.)

(At Rise: Interior of a bedroom at house on the campus at Legon, a shuttered room, a ceiling fan, a bed covered with mosquito netting, a shelf of books over a small writing table, and a delicate blue phonograph. All windows except one are shuttered. That window overlooks a winding road. The side of the room that is shuttered is dim. **SUZANNE ALEXANDER** *listens to a small radio. She is American, black, a pretty woman in her thirties. Part of her arm and shoulder are wrapped or bandaged in gauze. Placed on a shelf opposite her bed are a group of x-ray slides, the kind doctors use to analyze a patient's illness. She studies them, watches the road, and listlessly writes a line or so in a notebook. On the shelf is a photograph of Kwame Nkrumah, a book on Ludwig van Beethoven, a wedding photo of Suzanne and her husband, David, and a mural displaying various scenes of Ghana's independence.* **SUZANNE** *is dressed in a robe of kinte cloth.)*

(From outside Ghanaians play stringed musical instruments as they walk in an evening procession.)

SUZANNE. *(reads over notes from published diaries)* "The production of *Fidelio* was anticipated by months of increasing tension as the war with Napoleon escalated. Soldiers were quartered in all suburbs. At nine o'clock houses were locked and all inns cleared out. At Ulm on 20 October the Russians conceded defeat to the French. Ten days later, Bernadotte and the French army entered Salzburg. One saw baggage and travel-carriages passing. In the afternoon I went with Therese to the Danube. We saw the possessions of the Court being shipped off. The Court is sending everything away, even bedwarmers and shoetrees. It looks as if they have no intention of ever coming back to Vienna.

"After lunch Eppinger came with the devastating news that the Russians have retreated as far as Saint Polten. Vienna is in great danger of being swept over by marauding Chasseurs."

(SUZANNE suddenly turns to the radio.)

VOICE ON RADIO. I came into this world with the desire to give order to things: My one great hope was to be of the world and I discovered I was only an object among other objects. Sealed into that crushing objecthood I turned beseechingly to others. Their attention was a liberation endowing me once more with an agility that I had thought lost. But just as I reached the other side I stumbled and the movements, the attitudes, the glances of the others fixed me there. I burst apart. Now the fragments have been put together by another self.

ANOTHER VOICE ON THE RADIO. And that was David Alexander, the American professor of African poetry, here at the University…reading from Frantz Fanon. Mr. Alexander is still missing. Alexander traveled with Fanon in Blida. His wife, also American, the writer Suzanne Alexander, is recovering from an unspecified illness. It is known that she was writing a play about Ludwig van Beethoven when she was stricken. Alexander was by her side at the hospital when he suddenly vanished two nights ago. Mrs. Alexander has returned to their home on the campus at Legon near Accra.

(Musical passage of African stringed instruments.)

SUZANNE. *(reading from published diaries)* "The final rehearsal was on 22 May but the promised new overture was still in the pen of the creator. The orchestra was called to rehearsal in the morning of the performance. Beethoven did not come. After waiting a long time we drove to his lodgings to bring him bur he lay in bed sleeping soundly. Beside him stood a goblet with wine and a biscuit in it. The sheets of the overture were scattered on the floor and bed. A burnt out candle showed he had worked far into the night."

(The room appears out of the darkness. **SUZANNE** *rises and crosses to* **BEETHOVEN** *and stands staring at him.)*

RADIO. Although the couple are American they have lived in West Africa for a number of years and together started a newspaper that was a forerunner to Black Orpheus bringing together poems, stories, and novels by African writers as well as Afro-Americans, some in exile in England. It is known that often Alexander jests with his wife about her continued deep love for European artists such as Sibelius, Chopin, and Beethoven and indeed if anyone in Accra wants to hear these composers one has only to pass the windows of the delightful white stucco house among the fragrant flowers on the campus at Legon.

*(*SUZANNE *stares at* BEETHOVEN.*)*

SUZANNE. *(reading published notes from the diary)* "Beethoven was the the most celebrated of the living composers living in Vienna. The neglect of his person which he exhibited gave him a somewhat wild appearance. His features were strong and prominent; his eye was full of rude energy; his hair, which neither comb nor scissors seemed to have visited for years, overshadowed his broad brow in a quantity and confusion to which only the snakes round a Gorgon's head offer a parallel."

You worked into the night.

BEETHOVEN. Yes. Tonight is the opening of *Fidelio*.

SUZANNE. Did I awaken you?

BEETHOVEN. I was dreaming of my mother and how every year on Saint Magdalen's day, her name and birthdate, we would celebrate. The music stands would be brought out. And chairs would be placed everywhere and a canopy set up in the room where the portrait of my grandfather hung. We decorated the canopy with flowers, laurel branches, and foliage. Early in the evening my mother retired. And by ten o'clock everyone would be ready. The tuning up would begin and my mother would be awakened. She would then dress and be led in and seated in a beautifully decorated chair under the canopy. At that very moment magnificent music would strike up resounding throughout the neighborhood. And when the music ended, a meal was served and company ate and drank and danced until the celebration came to an end.

(loud voices from outside)

That must be the directors of the theater for the new overture. It's not finished.

*(**BEETHOVEN** starts toward the door and vanishes.)*

SUZANNE. Wait. I want to talk to you. Before David disappeared he questioned me on passages I wrote about you in Vienna. We argued.

*(She looks at drawings **BEETHOVEN** has in his room and sheet music on the floor. Suddenly she runs back to the open window watching the road for her husband. A long passage of the African stringed music from the procession on the road. **BEETHOVEN** returns and sits at the piano composing. He seems to have forgotten **SUZANNE**. She continues looking out of the window, listening to the African stringed music, watching the road for her husband, David. The music now changes into the overture **BEETHOVEN** is composing.)*

RADIO. Has Alexander been murdered?

SUZANNE. I've been unable to work. David helps me with all the scenes about you.

BEETHOVEN. Perhaps you might seek a retreat in the woods, Suzanne. It makes me happy to wander among herbs and trees.

(He continues composing music.)

SUZANNE. Tell me about your summers in Vienna... I have read life in Vienna during the hot months was not pleasant.

BEETHOVEN. Yes, like tonight here in Accra it was not pleasant. There were over a thousand horse-drawn cabs and over three hundred coaches of hire traveling across granite cobbles. They raised a terrible dust which hovered in the air the whole summer and even during part of the winter. It was like a dirty fog. I went to Baden and worked on a symphony.

SUZANNE. And your fame? I must ask you, are you happy with your fame?

BEETHOVEN. I do not like or have anything to do with people who refused to believe in me when I had not yet achieved fame. My three string quartets were all finished before fame came.

(He composes. She returns to the window. He composes music.)

SUZANNE. *(From diary)* "While he was working, he would stand at the washbasin and pour great pitchersful of water over his hands, at the same time howling the whole gamut of the scale, ascending and descending; then pace the room, his eyes fixed in a stare, jot down a few notes and again return to his water pouring and howling."

(music from Fidelio*)*

BEETHOVEN. You've argued about me?

SUZANNE. Yes. David says many scenes of you are too romantic-and that I must read more diaries about you. He gave me one by a Baron about this very room.

(reads to **BEETHOVEN***)*

SUZANNE. *(cont.)* "I wended my way to the unapproachable composer's home, and at the door it struck me that I had chosen the day ill, for, having to make an official visit thereafter, I was wearing the everyday habiliments of the Council of State. To make matters worse, his lodging was next to the city wall, and as Napoleon had ordered its destruction, blasts had just been set off under his windows."

RADIO. Has David Alexander been murdered? The outspoken professor at the University of Legon is still missing. As we have reported, Alexander worked with Fanon in Blida and was friends with the late Patrice Lumumba. Now that Fanon may be dying of cancer, Alexander has become highly vocal in keeping Fanon's words alive. We've played you his rendering of Fanon's essays and now we listen to David Alexander's poetry. It has never been dear, Alexander has said on many occasions, who the enemies of Fanon are and even though Ghana has won its independence, as Osegefo also continues to remind us: there are still enemies. Alexander was hated by many for his writing on the clinics and Fanon, and for his statements on the mental condition of the colonized patients. At first it was thought that when Alexander disappeared he was writing about one of the patients at the hospital at Legon, but now it has been revealed he was there waiting to hear the results of his wife's undisclosed surgery. And was indeed by her bedside and disappeared while she slept after surgery.

The Alexanders, an inseparable couple, often read their works together and have written a series of poems and essays jointly. It has been learned that at the hospital while sitting at his wife's side Alexander made sketches of his wife's illness and explained the progress and surgery procedures to her.

(Music. Passage that **BEETHOVEN** *is composing.)*

(From outside voices are heard shouting "Karl, Karl, Karl!" **BEETHOVEN** *rushes from the room.* **SUZANNE** *stands at the window. Music from the road blends with voices shouting, "Karl!"* **BEETHOVEN** *enters.)*

BEETHOVEN. My nephew Karl has tried to shoot himself. He's wounded. He's been taken to his mother's house.

SUZANNE. We'll go there.

BEETHOVEN. No. I can't. He told the police he was tormented by me and that is why he tried to kill himself and he does not want to see me. He says he's miserable and he's grown worse because I want him to live his life according to my expectation of him.

SUZANNE. *(writes in her manuscript)* Beethoven's nephew Karl tried to shoot himself. The tension between the two had reached a crisis. The incident left Beethoven in a shocked state. He was the only person Beethoven really loved to the point of idolatry.

RADIO. And again... Alexander...reading Fanon...still missing...where...has he been murdered?

SUZANNE. We could still walk to Karl's house near the Danube and look into his window. Perhaps you can call to him.

(Light in room fades. Now they are walking near the Danube. They look up at what could be Karl's windows.)

BEETHOVEN. *(shouts)* Karl, Karl, Karl!

(calls again)

Karl!

(long silence)

We've come far, Suzanne. We won't get back to Dobling until nearly four now.

SUZANNE. *(writing)* His nephew refused to see him. We did not get back to Dobling where Beethoven lived until seven. As we walked he started humming, sometimes howling, singing indefinite notes. "A theme for the last part of the overture has occurred to me," he said.

(Room appears again. **BEETHOVEN** *enters, running to the pianoforte. Music.)*

RADIO. *(David's voice reads an excerpt from Fanon.)* Yesterday awakening to the world I saw the sky utterly and wholly. I wanted to rise but fell paralyzed. Without responsibility nothingness, and infinitely I began to weep.

(Music. **BEETHOVEN** *composes.)*

SUZANNE. *(reads from the diary)* "Beethoven misunderstood me very often, and had to use the utmost concentration when I was speaking, to get my meaning. That, of course, embarrassed and disturbed me very much. It disturbed him, too, and this led him to speak more himself and very loudly. He told me a lot about his life and about Vienna. He was venomous and embittered. He raged about everything, and was dissatisfied with everything. He cursed Austria and Vienna in particular. He spoke quickly and with great vivacity. He often banged his fist on the piano and made such a noise that it echoed around the room."

*(***SUZANNE*** *writes while talking to* **BEETHOVEN**.*)*

You must dress now for the concert.

BEETHOVEN. Please go to the theater with me.

SUZANNE. I must watch the road for David.

BEETHOVEN. We'll stay together until David arrives. We'll watch the road and go to the theater together.

RADIO. An hour ago there was an accident near Kumasi that seemed to have some connection to Alexander but now that has been discounted.

It is now believed that David Alexander, learning of a plot against his life while he sat at his wife's bedside, chose to vanish to protect her, his colleague and fellow writer. Professor Alexander still continues to speak about attaining true independence. So now it is believed he is alive and waiting for the time when he can return home. Included in the next selection are two poems read by the couple together from their recording. The first selection is by Diop.

(radio fades)

BEETHOVEN. Is it true that David made drawings of your surgery as he sat by your side so that you would not be frightened?

SUZANNE. Yes.

BEETHOVEN. How very romantic. And do you believe that he vanished to protect you?

SUZANNE. Yes.

BEETHOVEN. And you compose poems and read together?

SUZANNE. Yes.

BEETHOVEN. What scenes did you fight over?

SUZANNE. He wanted a scene where you read your contracts, a scene where you talk about money.

*(***BEETHOVEN*** laughs.)*

BEETHOVEN. Do you disagree a great deal about your work together?

SUZANNE. No, only over this play. We set out to write it together years ago, then it became mine. Even on the morning of the surgery we argued about it.

*(***BEETHOVEN*** laughs.)*

BEETHOVEN. I feel David will return by morning, perhaps on the road with the musicians, perhaps even in disguise.

SUZANNE. Disguise.

BEETHOVEN. Yes.

RADIO. A body has been found in a swamp in Abijan. Is it Alexander? Has he been murdered?

*(***SUZANNE*** begins to unwrap her bandages.)*

BEETHOVEN. Why do you unwrap the gauze?

SUZANNE. The bandage is wrapped on my wound. I'm to unwrap it tonight and if the wound is pale white I'm still sick.

(BEETHOVEN starts to help her slowly unwrap the gauze. She does not look at her surgical wound as he unwraps the gauze.)

What color?

BEETHOVEN. The color is pale white.

(Silence.)

How long have you been sick?

SUZANNE. Two and one half years?

BEETHOVEN. You mustn't worry. I've foreseen my death many times. It will be in winter. In Vienna. My friends will come from Graz.

(He embraces her.)

(SUZANNE sits at BEETHOVEN's piano. He walks to the window.)

SUZANNE. *(reads from the diary)* "Before Beethoven's death I found him greatly disturbed and jaundiced all over his body. A frightful choleric attack had threatened his life the preceding night. Trembling and shivering he bent double because of the pains which raged in his liver and intestines; and his feet, hitherto moderately inflamed, were tremendously swollen. From this time on dropsy developed, the liver showed plain indication of hard nodules, there was an increase of jaundice. The disease moved onward with gigantic strides. Already in the third week there came incidents of nocturnal suffocation."

(radio)

VOICE ON RADIO. *(a recording of Alexander reading David Diop)*

Listen comrades of the struggling centuries

To the keen clamour of the Negro from Africa to the

Americas they have killed Mamba

As they killed the seven of Martinsville

or the Madagascan down there in the pale light of
the prisons...

(Room fades. They are backstage. **BEETHOVEN** *is dressed
formally for the theater. Music from stage. Orchestra
rehearsing Fidelio. They both watch the road.)*

SUZANNE. You must be happy tonight about *Fidelio.*

(He does not speak.)

BEETHOVEN. Suzanne, because of your anguish I want to
share a secret with you. For the last six years I have
been afflicted with an incurable complaint. From year
to year my hopes of being cured have gradually been
shattered and finally I have been forced to accept the
prospect of permanent infirmity. I am obliged to live
in solitude. If I try to ignore my infirmity I am cruelly
reminded of it. Yet I cannot bring myself to say to
people, "Speak up, shout, for I am deaf."

(music from stage, orchestra rehearsing Fidelio*)*

In the theater I have to place myself quite close to
the orchestra in order to understand what the actor
is saying, and at a distance I cannot hear the high
notes of instruments or voices. As for the spoken voice
it is surprising that some people have never noticed
my deafness; but since I have always been liable to fits
of absentmindedness, they attribute my hardness of
hearing to that. Sometimes, too, I can scarcely hear a
person who speaks softly; I can hear sounds, it is true,
but cannot make out the words. But if anyone shouts,
I can't bear it. I beg you not to say anything about my
condition to anyone. I am only telling you this as a
secret. Suzanne, if my trouble persists may I visit you
next spring?

SUZANNE. I had no idea you were going deaf.

BEETHOVEN. Yes, in fact you must write any further
questions in this little conversation book. I've been
trying to hide them from you.

(He gives her the conversation books.)

BEETHOVEN. You must write what you want to say to me in them. I cannot hear you.

SUZANNE. Ludwig!

(She embraces him.)

RADIO. *(**SUZANNE**'s voice reads from Fanon)* At the level of individuals violence is a cleansing force, it frees a man from despair and inaction.

It has been learned that the group who plotted to kill David Alexander has been discovered near Kumasi and has been arrested. It is safe for Alexander to return to Accra. And it is reported that Nkrumah himself met with the revolutionary poet a few hours ago and reported to him the details of his would-be assassins' capture.

SUZANNE. *(suddenly)* Ludwig, why is David's handwriting in your conversation books? This poem is in David's own handwriting.

*(**BEETHOVEN** does not answer.)*

*(**SUZANNE** studies the conversation books.)*

Ludwig! There is a message from David, a love poem of Senghor's. Whenever David wants to send me a message he puts a poem inside my papers, in a book he knows I will read.

(She writes in conversation book and reads.)

Be not astonished, my love, if at times my song grows dark

If I change my melodious reed for the khalam and the tama's beat

And the green smell of the rice fields for galloping rumble of the tabalas.

Listen to the threats of old sorcerers, to the thundering wrath of God!

Ah, maybe tomorrow the purple voice of your songmaker will be silent forever.

That's why today my song is so urgent and my fingers bleed on my khalam.

(She opens another conversation book. Music from the stage.)

(reads David's words)

Suzanne, please continue writing scenes. Please continue writing scenes we talked about.

(Lights fade backstage and come up on concert hall. **BEETHOVEN** *now stands before the orchestra, stage center. He waves baton wildly. It is obvious he does not hear. Music stops. He starts again. He waves wildly, throwing the singers and orchestra off beat and into confusion. Silence. He calls* **SUZANNE** *to his side. She writes in the book.* **BEETHOVEN** *buries his face and rushes to the wings leaving the orchestra.* **SUZANNE** *writes.)*

Ludwig was still desperately trying to conduct in public and insisted upon conducting rehearsals even though by now during the concert the orchestra knew to ignore his beat and to follow instead the Kapellmeister who stood behind him.

*(***BEETHOVEN** *returns stage center. As she speaks* **BEETHOVEN** *conducts. Music.)*

SUZANNE. *(cont.)* At *Fidelio* Ludwig waved his baton back and forth with violent motions, not hearing a note. If he thought it should be piano, he crouched down almost under the podium and if he wanted faster he jumped up with strange gestures uttering strange sounds. Yet the evening was a triumph.

*(***SUZANNE** *stands at window writing. A shadow appears on the road.)*

David!

*(The deaf **BEETHOVEN** turns to her, smiles, conducting violently. Music.)*

(reads from the diary)

"As for the musical success of this memorable evening, it could be favorably compared to any event ever presented in that venerable theatre, Alas, the man to whom all this honor was addressed could hear none of it, for when at the end of the performance the audience broke into enthusiastic applause, he remained standing with his back to them, Then the contralto soloist had the presence of mind to turn the master toward the proscenium and show him the cheering throng throwing their hats into the air and waving their handkerchiefs, He acknowledged his gratitude with a bow, This set off an almost unprecedented volley of jubilant applause that went on and on as the joyful listeners sought to express their thanks for the pleasure they had just been granted."

*(Concert scene fades to **BEETHOVEN**'s room. **SUZANNE** stands in the center staring at **BEETHOVEN**'s grand piano, his chair, manuscript paper.)*

(reads from the diary)

"Monday, the 26th of March 1827 was a freezing day, From Silesia and the Sudeten peaks, a north wind blew across the Wienerwald. Everywhere the ground lay under a soft blanket of fresh, silent snow. The long winter had been raw, damp, cold, and frosty; on that day it showed no sign of releasing its grip on the land.

By four o'clock the lights of Vienna, the street lamps, the candles of myriad rooms, began to pierce the overcast gloom, On the second floor of the Schwarzspanierhaus, the House of the Black Spaniard, to the west of the old city walls, lay a man who had all but run his course, In a large, sparsely furnished room of 'sad appearance,' amid squalor and books and manuscript paper and within sight of his prized mahogany Broadwood grand, Beethoven lost hold of life. On a roughly made bed, unconscious, he was at that moment as broken and finished as his piano. The elements continued to rage. Flurries of snow drifted against the window. Then, there was suddenly, a loud clap of thunder accompanied by a bolt of lightning... Beethoven opened his eyes, raised his right hand, and, his fist clenched, looked upward for several seconds... As he let his hand sink down onto the bed again, his eyes half closed... There was no more breathing, no more heartbeat! The great composer's spirit fled from this world."

So remembered Anselm Huttenbrenner, who recorded Beethoven's end even more poignantly in the terseness of a diary entry: "Ludwig van Beethoven's death, in the evening, toward six o'clock of dropsy in his fifty-seventh year. He is no longer!"

(She cries. Music from the road, of African stringed instruments. **SUZANNE** *rushes to the door.)*

David. You sent Beethoven until you returned. Didn't you?

DAVID'S VOICE. *(not unlike* **BEETHOVEN***'s)* I knew he would console you while I was absent.

END

1964. Courtesy of the author

Adrienne Kennedy continues to influence the world through her art. She was the recipient of the 2003 Lifetime Achievement Award from the Anisfield-Wolf Book Awards, an Obie Award for Lifetime Achievement Award, the Lila Wallace—Reader's Digest Writers' Award and the American Academy of Arts and Letters in Literature Award. She was also granted a Guggenheim Fellowship for Creative Writing, awarded the Pierre Lecomte du Novy Award, and ended her academic career teaching at Harvard.

Kennedy was playwright-in-residence at the Signature Theatre in New York City during their 1996-1997 season. Her play *Movie Star* is in a volume of Norton Anthology of American Literature and her play *Funnyhouse of Negro*, most recently performed at the Classical Theatre of Harlem in NYC, is a landmark piece that speaks to students trying to find a place in the world.

Her plays are taught in classrooms and performed in theatres all over the world.